agate

What good is a moose?

Joy Morgan Dey

Nikki Johnson

First Edition: April 2007

LAKE SUPERIOR PORT CITIES INC.
P.O. Box 16417
Duluth, Minnesota 55816-0417 USA
1-888-BIG LAKE (888-244-5253)
www.lakesuperior.com
Publishers of *Lake Superior Magazine* and *Lake Superior Travel Guide*

5 4 3 2 1

Dey, Joy Morgan 1945-
Johnson, Nikki 1948-
    Agate / by Joy Morgan Dey; Illustrations by Nikki Johnson. – 1st ed.
    48p. 26cm.

ISBN 0-942235-73-8
ISBN 978-0-942235-73-9

1. Agate – Fiction. 2. Gemstones. 3. Birthstones.
4. Self-esteem. I. Title.

Library of Congress Catalog Number 2007921080

            Editor: Konnie LeMay
Cover & Book Design: Joy Morgan Dey
        Illustrations: Nikki Johnson

Printed in Singapore

What good is a moose?

Agate thinks to himself,
As he mopes at the edge of a lake.
He looks like a Tinker Toy project gone wrong,
He feels like a big brown mistake.

He thinks of his friends as sparkling gems,
Beautiful, talented, bright.
Oh, how he'd love to shine like them.
Agate sighs. It just isn't right.

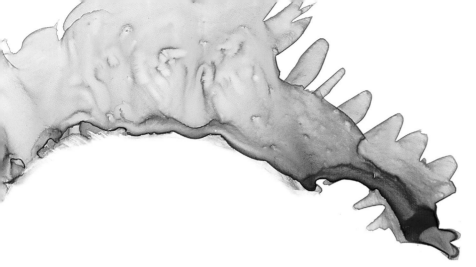

A major star in the film Peter Pan, this guy is famous for smiles.

Agate's lopsided grin

could scarcely compare

with **Garnet**

the crocodile's.

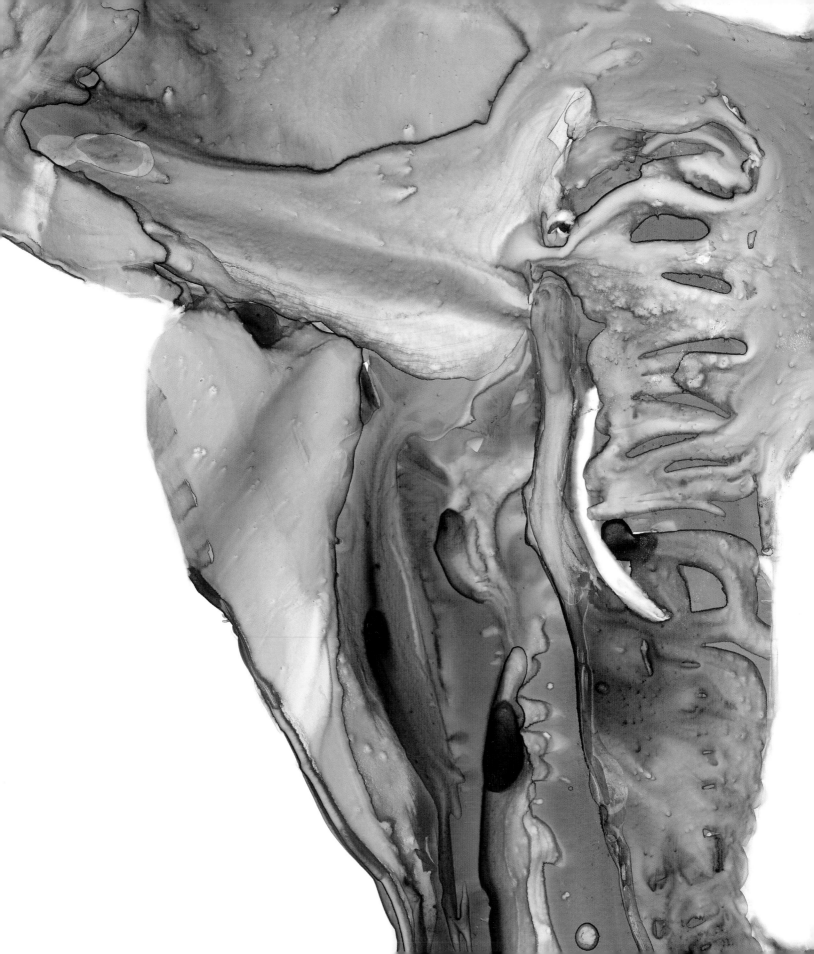

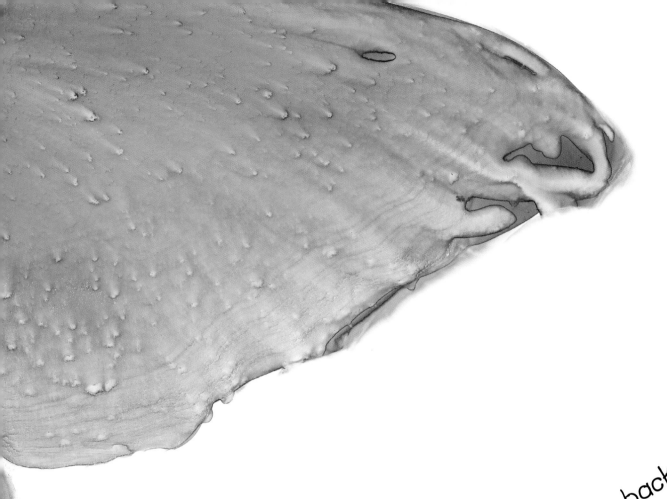

With a built-in squirt gun for spraying her back

And gigantic fans for ears,

Five-ton **Amethyst** always stays cool.

She'll live 80 tremendous years.

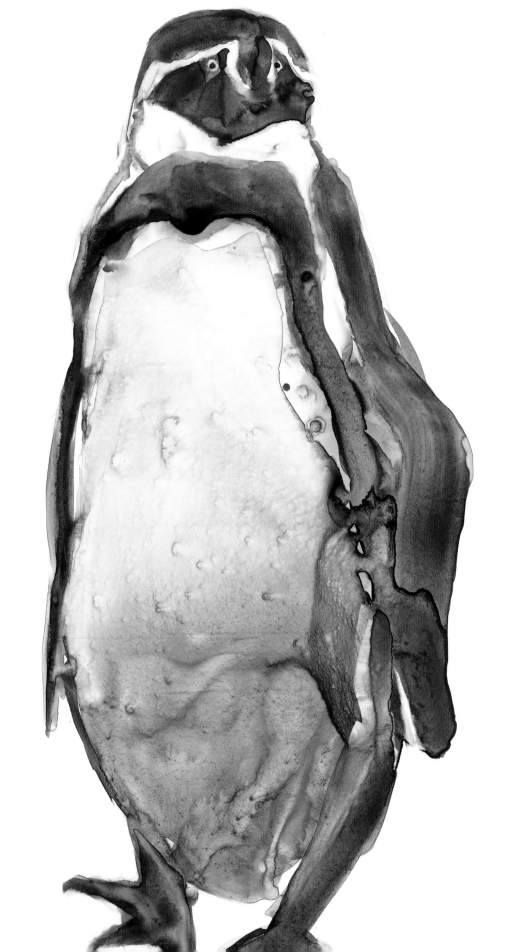

The sea provides his sushi bar,

His drinking water, too.

Aquamarine surfs and dives,

Enjoying his ocean view.

What good is a moose?

Compared to such gems,
Agate feels like a nondescript rock.
Too big, with loose lips and knobbly knees,
Each leg like rocks in a sock.

Diamond reaches food that no one else can.

He sees for miles, he's so tall.

With his long, long legs, he can run really fast.

Agate feels awkward and small.

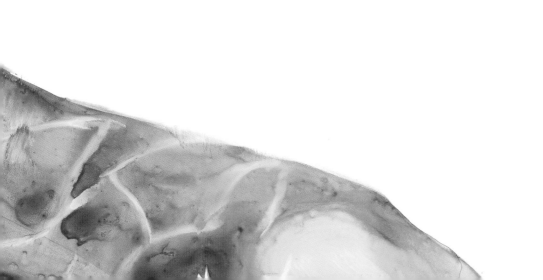

Emerald has muscle as well as good looks,

Like a Porsche with a Hemi inside.

What's to fear when you're strong as Hercules,

And the word

for your family

is PRIDE?

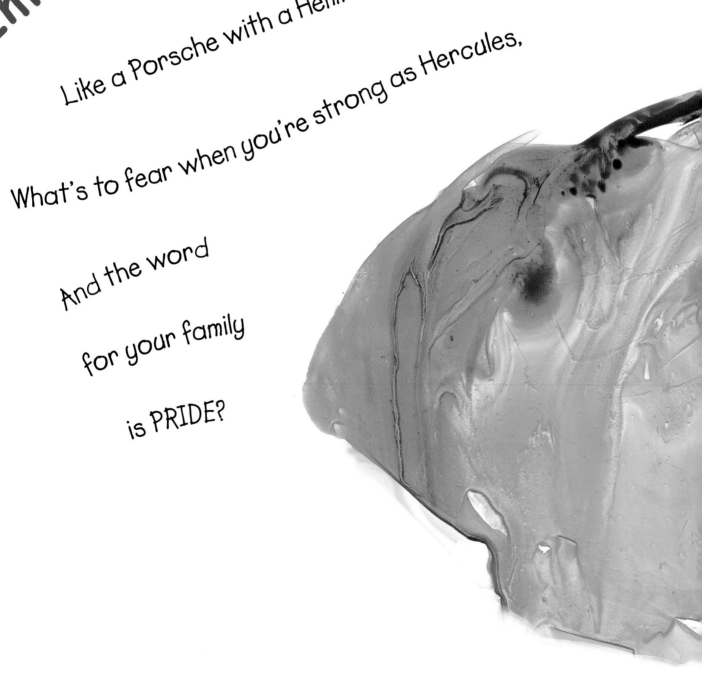

Arm over arm, **Pearl** playfully swings,

Leaping from tree to tree.

She plays practical jokes on all sorts of folks,

Hm-m-m . . . What will her <u>next</u> trick be?

Agate shuffles away, feeling low as can be,
Clumsy, disjointed and loose.
Not for the first time, he thinks to himself —
Really!

What good is a moose?

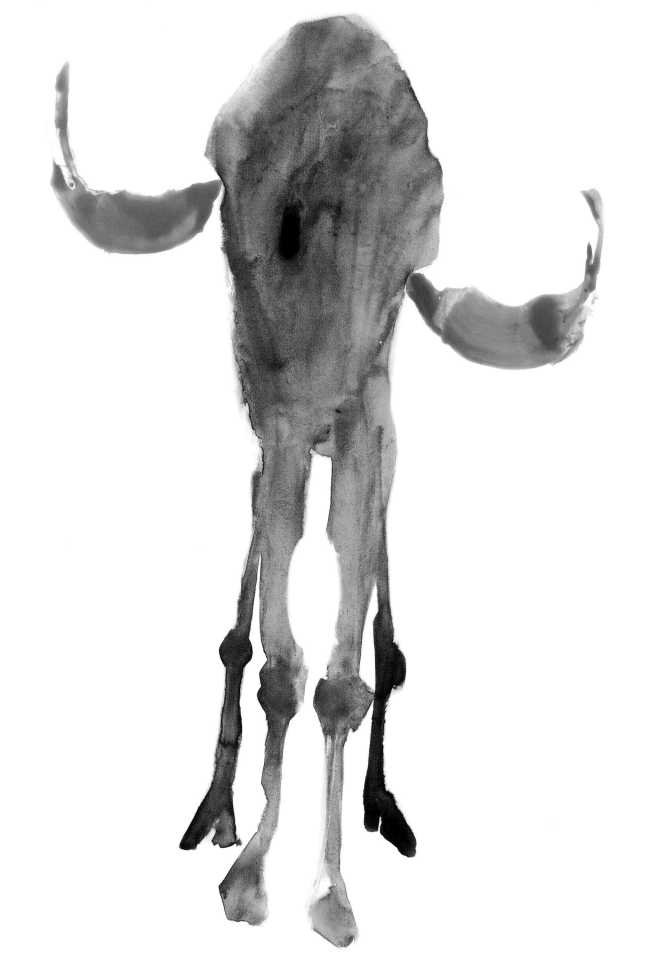

Ruby red bears gracefully waltz

to that 1-2-3, 1-2-3 beat.

Agate loves watching, but he won't join in —

Afraid he would have four left feet.

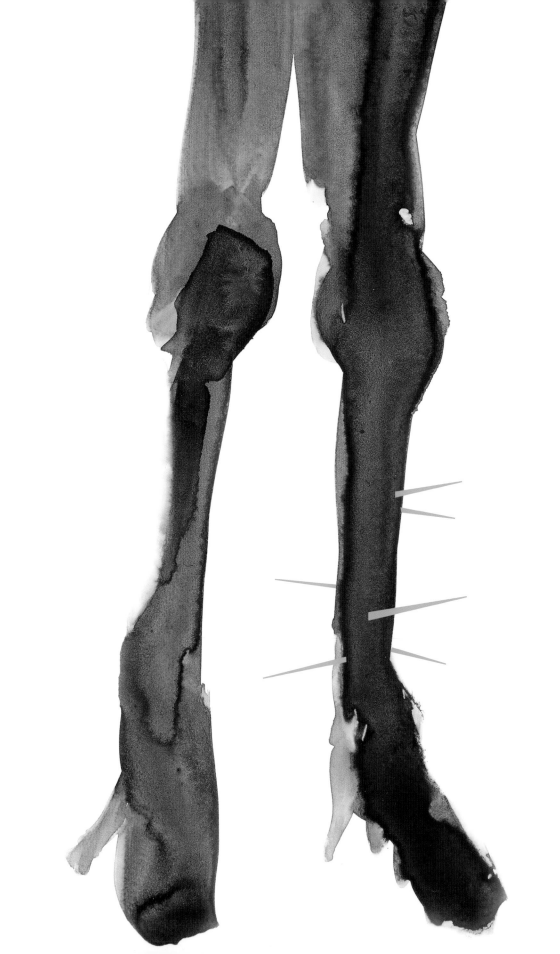

Her beautiful quills are a statement of fashion,

But don't get in Peridot's face.

A flick of her tail

is all that it takes

To maintain her

personal space.

Webbed feet are all this superb swimmer needs.

Why bother with a bikini?

Sapphire stays under six minutes or so —

Longer than Harry Houdini.

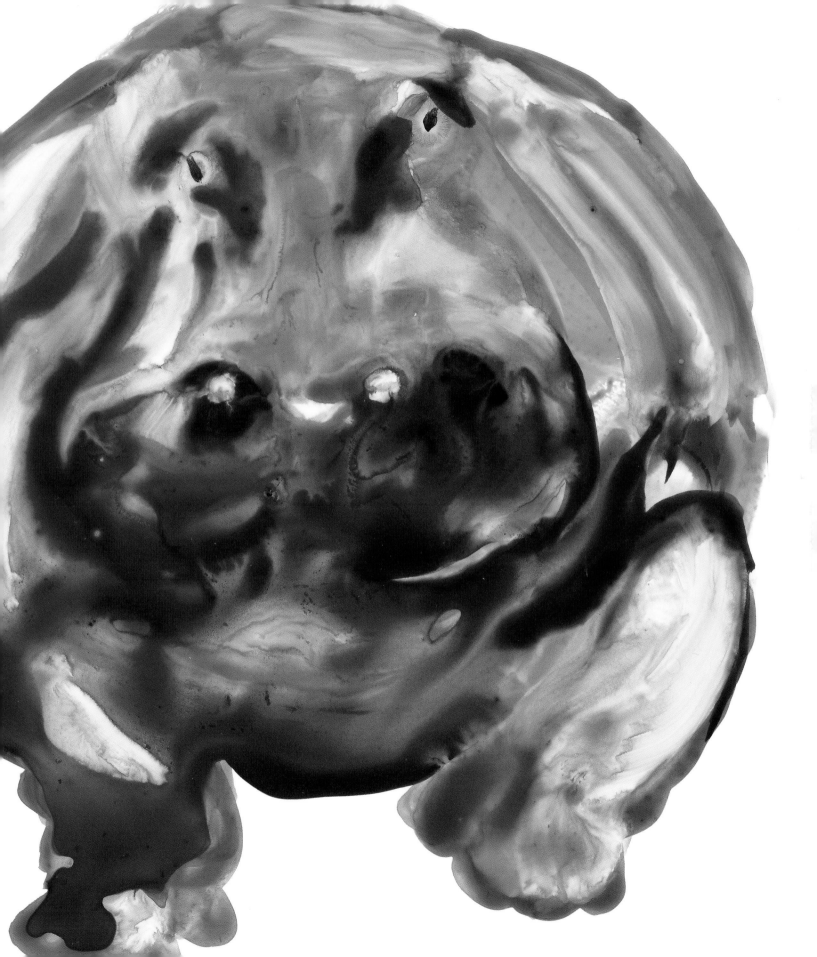

Agate could use some polish, it's true,
To bring out the beauty inside.

What good is a moose?

He hasn't a clue.
He looks for a good place to hide.

She likes berries or fish or some compost-pile dish —

Opal's <u>not</u> a finicky eater.

She can open a garbage can lid or a gate,

Going anywhere mischief will lead her.

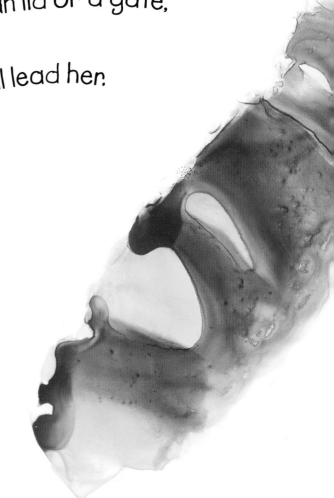

Agate knows he will never soar like an eagle.

Look at those strong wings and beak.

Obviously, Topaz doesn't have doubts,

Or feel shy

Or silly

Or weak.

Turquoise eats bugs, 600 an hour.

He uses his hearing for steering.

How cool is that? – Agate's impressed.

What a marvel of fine engineering!

But what good is a moose?!

Agate's almost in tears.
His friends see he really is blue.
You're just like us, Agate, you big galoot.
If <u>we</u> are gems, so are <u>you</u>.

Just do what you're good at,
like being a moose,
And remember this simple rule:
Let yourself shine,
and let others find . . .

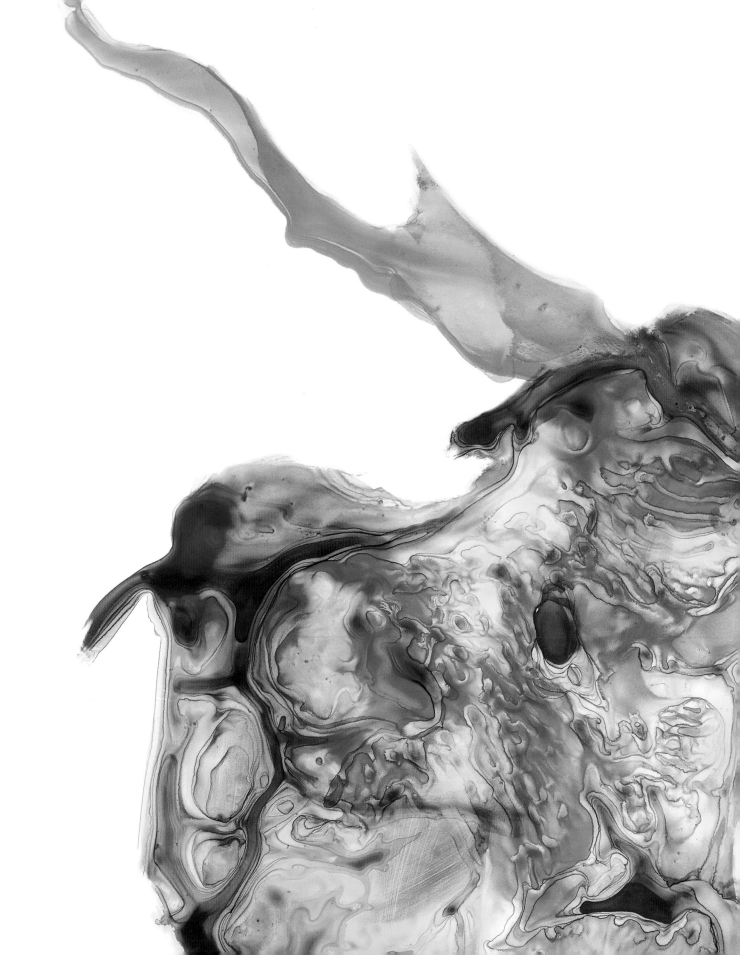

A moose, like an unpolished agate, is plain,
Yet unique, with a beautiful heart.
Let **Agate** share with you what he has learned –
For a self-conscious moose, it's a start . . .

We're a malcontented bunch –
Give us breakfast, we want lunch.
Give us flippers, we want paws.
Show us talents, we see flaws.
Make us tall, we'd rather be small.
Give us some, we want it all.
Comparison can help us grow,
But a little is enough, and so . . .

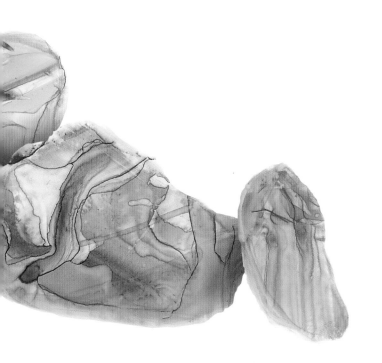

Be glad they're them
and you
are you . . .

. . . each a gem in life's marvelous zoo!

Agate, the Secret Jewel

Agates are nature's hidden artwork. The rough, plain surface forms first, hiding the beautiful rings of crystals that grow one layer at a time toward the center. Bands of color make each agate a work of art. No wonder agates have names like cloud, lace, fire, moss, picture, rainbow and tree.

Agates can be found all over the world, but the best ones usually come from Brazil, Uruguay or the United States. Agate is the state gemstone, mineral or rock of Arizona, Kentucky, Louisiana, Minnesota, Montana, Nebraska, South Dakota and Tennessee in the United States and of the province of Nova Scotia in Canada. An agate can be as small as a pea or as large as a bowling ball.

Agates have been used as jewelry and other decorations and as bowls for thousands of years. Children's marbles called "aggies" were made of agate not so long ago. Many museums have examples of gorgeous agates, including the Smithsonian in Washington, D.C., and the Louvre in Paris, which has spectacular agate bowls.

According to folklore, agates can help you get in touch with nature, see the world with a broader viewpoint and have pleasant dreams. If you go out looking for agates, all of these claims might come true!

This Lake Superior agate is from the collection of Terry Roses, Fragments of History, Duluth, Minnesota.

Everybody Has a Birthstone

Why do we have birthstones? Do you know which one is yours? There is a special gemstone for each month of the year, so whatever month you were born in, that's your birthstone.

The idea of birthstones is thousands of years old. They were once connected with the signs of the Zodiac and even with the 12 tribes of Israel in the Bible. Different traditions use different stones. Below are today's most popular choices. Over the years, people passed along myths and legends about gems, giving them magical powers. They thought that wearing these stones could make them healthy or happy or safe. Some used gems for healing, grinding them up then eating the powder or soaking them then drinking the water. Medicine has come a long way, but people still like to believe that wearing birthstones will bring good luck and help keep them safe.

January ◆ Garnet
(or Rose Quartz)

Garnet actually refers to a whole family of gemstones, which come in every color of the spectrum except blue. The violet-red variety is the best known. It is the gem of faith, constancy and truth.

February ◆ Amethyst
(or Onyx)

Because of their rich, royal color, amethysts have sometimes been reserved for wear only by the nobility. They are used both polished and unpolished. Brazil and Zambia are today's main sources.

March ◆ Aquamarine
(or Bloodstone)

In Latin, "aquamarine" means sea water. Sailors wore this gem, the color of the sea, to protect them. Aquamarine is the gem of friendship, harmony and trust. It is mined in Nigeria, Pakistan, Madagascar and Mozambique, but the finest aquamarines are found in Brazil.

April ◆ Diamond
(or Rock Crystal)

Diamonds, the hardest substance on earth, are crystallized carbon, brought up to the earth's surface by volcanoes. Hindus believed diamonds were created by lightning and the people of Greece thought they were fragments of stars. Diamonds are usually sparkling clear, but they can also be green, yellow, orange, pink or blue. Most diamonds today are found in Australia, the Soviet Union and Africa. The diamond symbolizes everlasting love.

May ◆ Emerald
(or Chrysoprase)

The intense green color of emeralds (picture the Emerald City in *The Wizard of Oz)* comes from traces of chromium or vanadium. The most famous deposits are in Columbia. Emeralds are supposed to be good for just about anything from curing snakebite to promoting courage and honesty.

June ◆ Pearl
(or Moonstone or Alexandrite)

The people of Greece thought that pearls were tears of joy from the goddess of love. Arabs once thought that they were moonlit dewdrops swallowed by oysters. And the Chinese thought that they came from dragon brains. Today, we know that mollusks create pearls around irritating grains of sand to smooth things out. This takes many years, so pearls formed in this way cost thousands of dollars. Natural pearls are found in the Persian Gulf and in the waters off Japan, the South Pacific islands, Panama, Venezuela and California.

September ◆ Sapphire
(or Lapis)

Sapphires symbolize truth. Ancient Persians believed that a huge sapphire supported the earth and that reflections from it caused the blue of the sky. In star sapphires, light is reflected in such a way that a star seems to float across the stone as it is moved. The 543-carat Star of India is on display at the American Museum of Natural History in New York City.

November ◆ Topaz
(or Citrine)

Topaz comes in a wide range of colors. The name comes either from the Sanskrit word for "fire" or from the island of Topazos in the Red Sea. Topaz is associated with strength. Important sources of topaz are Brazil, Russia, Siberia, Australia and Mexico, and New Hampshire, Colorado and Utah in the United States.

July ◆ Ruby
(or Carnelian)

Rubies are very hard, second only to diamonds. Sometimes they are used in watches to protect moving parts. This symbol of freedom, dignity and divine power is among the royal jewels of many nations. Most rubies come from Burma today, although they are produced in several other countries, including the United States in North Carolina.

August ◆ Peridot
(or Sardonyx)

Peridot came from St. John's Island in the Red Sea for 3,500 years. Egyptians called it "the gem of the sun," saying it was invisible in daylight and could only be found at night by its inner glow. Today, Burma is its main source. Peridots have even been found in meteorites.

October ◆ Opal
(or Tourmaline)

Shakespeare referred to opal as "the queen of gems." Layers of silica spheres break up light into a dramatic rainbow of colors – all the colors of the other birthstones, in fact. No wonder opal symbolizes hope. A dry, barren corner of Australia holds the world's most important source of opal. It is mined on a small scale, often by hand, even using only a pocket knife.

December ◆ Turquoise (or Tanzanite or Zircon)

People around the world have long treasured turquoise, considered to be a sign of health and prosperity. Today it is principally produced in the southwestern United States – New Mexico, Nevada and Arizona. We tend to picture the blue-green variety with the spider web pattern of veins in the surrounding rock or matrix.

Special thanks to . . .

Paul and Cindy Hayden, for graciously heeding the call of destiny.

Don and Nancy Tubesing, for so serendipitously paving the way.

Anita Zager, always generous in her support of all things literary.

Kathy Halverson, a teacher, who spends her days polishing little gems.

Family and friends, who somehow manage to give both

helpful criticism and unfailing support.